The Mysterious Guests

A *Sukkot* Story

by Eric A. Kimmel

illustrated by
Katya Krenina

Holiday House / New York

Printed in the United States of America

The text typeface is Breughel.

The artwork was created with acrylics.

www.holidayhouse.com

First Edition

1 3 5 7 9 10 8 6 4 2

Library of Congress Cataloging-in-Publication Data

Kimmel, Eric A.

The mysterious guests : a Sukkot story / by Eric A. Kimmel ;

illustrated by Katya Krenina.—1st ed.

p. cm.

Summary: Three mysterious guests appear at generous but impoverished Ezra's table on
Sukkot and bless him, while they bring curses upon his rich but selfish brother Eben.

ISBN 978-0-8234-1893-0 (hardcover)

[1. Fairy tales. 2. Sukkot—Fiction.] I. Krenina, Katya, ill. II. Title.

PZ8.K527My 2008

[E]—dc22

2007043208

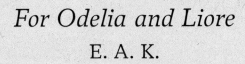

For Odelia and Liore
E. A. K.

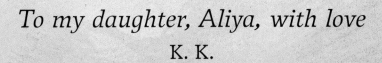

To my daughter, Aliya, with love
K. K.

It is said that the three forefathers, Abraham, Isaac, and Jacob, return to Earth for the harvest festival of Sukkot. Disguised as weary travelers, they appear at the sukkah, asking to share the holiday meal. If they are welcomed as honored guests, they leave a blessing. If not, they teach a lesson that is not soon forgotten.

Two brothers once lived in the land of Israel. Eben, the elder, was extremely rich and extremely selfish. His name means "stone," and he lived up to it, for he cared no more about others than he did for the stones lying beside the road.

His brother, Ezra, was kind and generous. His name means "help," and he lived up to it too. Although Ezra was as poor as his brother, Eben, was rich, he treated all as if they were members of his own family. He never hesitated to share what little he had with those in need.

Every year when the holiday of Sukkot arrived, Eben built a magnificent sukkah. Its boards were fragrant cedar. Fresh-smelling pine and juniper boughs covered its roof. Pears, apples, and grapes at the peak of ripeness decorated the sukkah from top to bottom.

Every meal in the sukkah was like a royal banquet, for Eben would allow only the finest delicacies to be served at his table. His guests were the most important people in the land. They ate from gold dishes and drank from silver cups.

Poor people sometimes approached Eben's sukkah. It would have been a sin to turn them away. However, Eben never allowed them to feel welcome. He never invited them to sit at the table. They had to stand in a corner, away from the other guests. They could look on and admire, but they were not permitted to touch anything. After the banquet Eben gave them the leftovers. He called this "charity."

Only the poorest people accepted Eben's "charity." It made them feel like beggars.

Ezra's sukkah was not nearly as grand as his brother's. Its boards were bits and pieces of scrap lumber collected over the years. Its boughs were fallen palm branches. Ezra could not afford to buy ripe fruits. He decorated his sukkah with leaves and wildflowers. He searched the marketplace for overripe pears, apples, and bunches of grapes that were about to be thrown away. Ezra could buy a whole basket of these for a few coins. He discarded the rotten grapes and cut the spoiled parts from the pears and apples so that when he hung these fruits from the roof and walls of his sukkah, they looked as beautiful as the ones his brother, Eben, hung from his.

Ezra welcomed all who came to his
sukkah. He never turned anyone away.
Rich and poor sat together at the table.
Everyone brought something to share:
a loaf of bread, a fresh salad, a bowl of
yogurt, fresh cheese made from sheep's or
goat's milk, a bouquet of flowers, a new
song, or an interesting story.

Everyone, no matter how poor, had something to bring. Ezra might not have been as wealthy as his brother, but in his sukkah there was always enough to go around. In truth, people preferred Ezra's sukkah to Eben's. Joy and friendship filled Ezra's sukkah. Pride and vanity filled Eben's.

Abraham, Isaac, and Jacob came down from heaven on the eve of Sukkot. With dusty cloaks on their backs and worn-out sandals on their feet, they wandered from town to town. Stopping at every sukkah, they asked to be invited in. They were always welcomed.

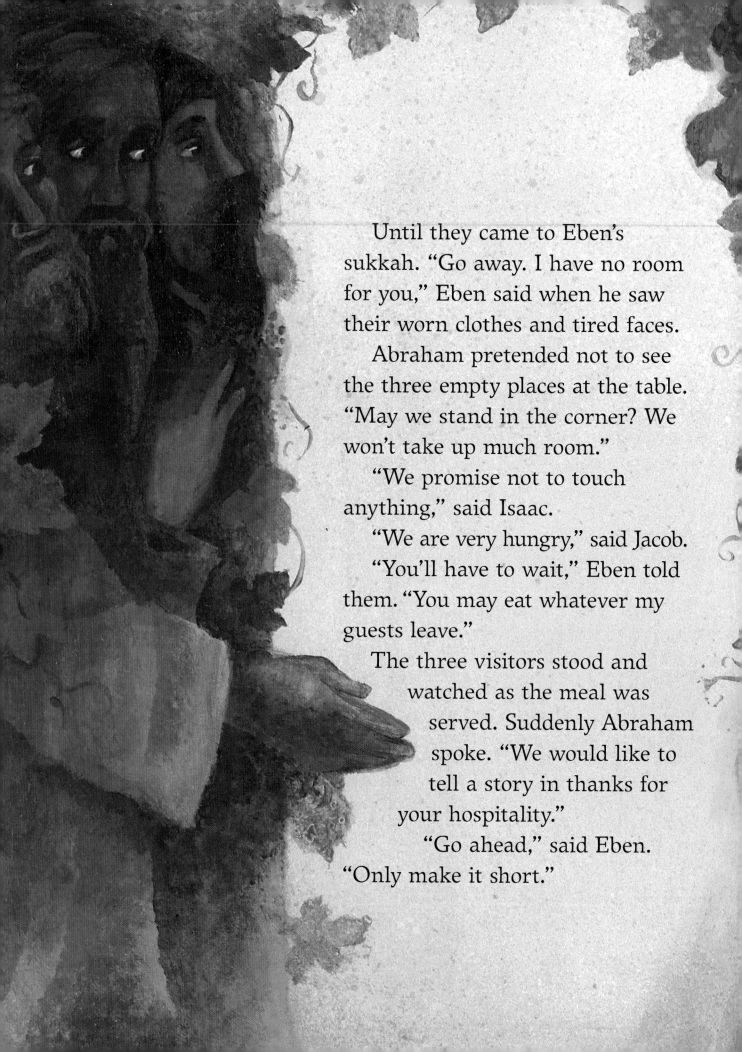

Until they came to Eben's sukkah. "Go away. I have no room for you," Eben said when he saw their worn clothes and tired faces.

Abraham pretended not to see the three empty places at the table. "May we stand in the corner? We won't take up much room."

"We promise not to touch anything," said Isaac.

"We are very hungry," said Jacob.

"You'll have to wait," Eben told them. "You may eat whatever my guests leave."

The three visitors stood and watched as the meal was served. Suddenly Abraham spoke. "We would like to tell a story in thanks for your hospitality."

"Go ahead," said Eben. "Only make it short."

"There was once a man who built a beautiful sukkah. Its boards were cedar. Its boughs, fresh-cut pine and juniper," Isaac began.

"But all the beauty was on the outside," Jacob continued. "The inside was rotten with selfishness. The man had no room in his sukkah for kindness or charity. One day three visitors came to the sukkah. The man treated them as beggars. He would not allow them to sit at the table. He did not offer them food or drink. When the meal was over, the three visitors departed. As they left, they spoke a special blessing."

"May this sukkah's outside be like its inside," said Abraham.

"What is the point of this ridiculous story?" Eben snapped.

Isaac and Jacob answered, "Look around. You will see."

Eben and his guests looked up. The beautiful fruits hanging from the roof and walls of the sukkah turned rotten before their eyes. Black mold spread across the apples. White fungus covered the grapes.

Worms crawled out of the pears. Toads, snakes, lizards—a host of creeping things— swarmed out of the fruits and began falling onto the table. They plopped into the soup. They burrowed into the bread. They crawled, hopped, and slithered across the golden plates. They dropped onto the guests' laps and into their jeweled, perfumed hair. Eben's guests ran screaming from the sukkah.

"What is the meaning of this?" Eben shouted at the three visitors. As he spoke, they vanished.

Soon afterward the same three travelers came to Ezra's sukkah. "May we come in?" they asked.

"Of course. I am happy to have you. Everyone is welcome in this sukkah," Ezra replied.

The people at the table made room for the new guests. They brought food for them to eat and filled their cups with wine. The three visitors joined the feasting.

When all had finished, Ezra said, "It is the custom for each of my guests to bring something to the sukkah. It might be food to eat. It might be a song, a bit of news, a clever riddle. Might our three visitors have something to share with the rest of us?"

"Indeed we do," said Abraham. "We have a story to tell."

"Then let us hear it."

Abraham began. "Once there was a man who was good and kind. He greeted everyone who came to his sukkah. He shared what little he had. He made the poorest people feel welcome. The generosity that filled the man's sukkah was as precious as silver and gold."

"One day three strangers approached the sukkah," said Isaac. "The man invited them to his table. He treated them as honored guests. When the visitors departed, they left a special blessing."

"May this sukkah's outside be like its inside," said Jacob.

"What a strange story. What does it mean?" asked Ezra.

"Look around. You will see."

Ezra and his guests looked at
the sukkah's walls. They stared up
at its roof. All the fruits and flowers
hanging there had turned to silver. All
the limbs and boughs turned to gold.

"Who are you? I know you are not
part of this world!" Ezra cried.

But the mysterious guests
had vanished.

From that day on Ezra became a wealthy man. Good fortune followed him so that he soon became even more prosperous than his brother, Eben. Every year at Sukkot, he built a magnificent sukkah, the most beautiful in the land, where every person, rich or poor, was welcomed as an honored guest.

As for Eben, he searched his heart and changed his ways. Every year he too built a beautiful sukkah, to which he welcomed all who came. And if the fruits and flowers of his sukkah never turned to gold or silver, neither did they bring forth toads and lizards.

AUTHOR'S NOTE

The Jewish harvest festival of Sukkot dates back three thousand years. It is mentioned in the Bible in Leviticus 23: 33-36. On Sukkot, the Israelites brought the first fruits of their harvest to the Temple in Jerusalem.

The holiday takes its name from the Hebrew word *sukkot*, meaning booths, sheds, or temporary structures. (A single structure is called a *sukkah*.) The ancient Israelites stayed out in the fields, living in sukkot until the harvest was gathered. Today, traditional Jewish families live in sukkot for the eight days of the holiday, whether or not they are involved in agriculture. Sukkot can be found on fire escapes in major cities as well as in fields in the countryside.

Kindness and hospitality to strangers and guests is of paramount importance in the Jewish religion. The book of Genesis tells how God Himself visited Abraham's camp disguised as a stranger to announce the birth of Isaac and the destruction of Sodom (Genesis 18:1-33). Opening the door to welcome the prophet Elijah is one of the main parts of the Passover Seder. Ancient traditions also tell how Abraham, his son Isaac, and Isaac's son Jacob, the ancestors of the Jewish people, visit each sukkah as guests. They bestow blessings wherever they are welcomed.